Locust Plague

Julie Haydon

Australia • Brazil • Japan • Korea • Mexico • Singapore • Spain • United Kingdom • United States

Locust Plague

Fast Forward
Gold Level 21

Text: Julie Haydon
Illustrations: Boris Silvestri
Editor: Rebecca Quinn
Design: James Lowe
Series design: James Lowe
Production controller: Seona Galbally
Photo research: Fiona Smith
Audio recordings: Juliet Hill, Picture Start
Spoken by: Matthew King and Abbe Holmes
Reprint: Jennifer Foo

Acknowledgements

The author and publisher thank Dr Martin Steinbauer of the Australian Plague Locust Commission for his expert advice. The author and publisher would also like to acknowledge permission to reproduce material from the following sources: Photographs by Alamy/FLPA, pp back cover, 16; ANT Photo Library, 10 left; ANT Photo Library/Otto Rogge, pp front cover, 1, 4 left, 4 inset, 4 right, 5, 8 left, 8 right, 9; Commonwealth Copyright of Australia/Australian Government Department of Agriculture, Fisheries and Forestry/Australian Plague Locust Commission, p 7; Corbis/John & Lorraine Carnemolla, p 17; Corbis/Eric and David Hosking, p 23; Corbis/Sygma/Patrick Robert, pp 13, 22 right, 22 bottom; Fairfaxphotos/Nick Moir, pp 10 right, 11; iStockphoto.com/Imad ud Din, p 14 inset; iStockphoto.com/Kevin Russ, p 14; iStockphoto.com/Moritz von Hacht, p 15; Nature Picture Library/Adrian Davies, p 22 left; Newspix, p 20–21; Newspix/Chris Crerar, pp 12 centre, 12 bottom; Newspix/Dean Martin, p 18; Newspix/Jeff Darmanin, p 19; Newspix/John Grainger, p 6; illustration by Boris Silvestri, p 7.

ISBN 978 0 17 012678 6
ISBN 978 0 17 012669 4 (set)

Cengage Learning Australia
Level 7, 80 Dorcas Street
South Melbourne, Victoria Australia 3205
Phone: 1300 790 853

Cengage Learning New Zealand
Unit 4B Rosedale Office Park
331 Rosedale Road, Albany, North Shore NZ 0632
Phone: 0508 635 766

For learning solutions, visit cengage.com.au

Printed in Australia by Ligare Pty Ltd
6 7 8 9 10 11 12 21 20 19 18 17

THE UNIVERSITY OF MELBOURNE

Evaluated in independent research by staff from the Department of Language, Literacy and Arts Education at the University of Melbourne.

Locust Plague

Julie Haydon

Contents

Chapter 1

WHAT ARE LOCUSTS?

Locusts are insects that look like grasshoppers. They have wings and large back legs for jumping. There are different kinds, or **species**, of locusts. Locusts are found in many countries around the world.

an Australian plague locust

Locusts eat plants.
Many species of locusts feed on different kinds of grass, but some locusts will eat any green plant, especially when grass is hard to find or there are lots of locusts.

Life Cycle of a Locust

Locusts have three life cycle stages – egg, **nymph** and adult.

First, female locusts lay their eggs in the ground. Then, baby locusts, called nymphs or hoppers, hatch from the eggs.

locust nymphs

When a nymph hatches,
it has **wing pads**, but no wings.
Nymphs go through many growth stages
before they become adults.
Finally, at the adult stage,
the wing pads become wings.

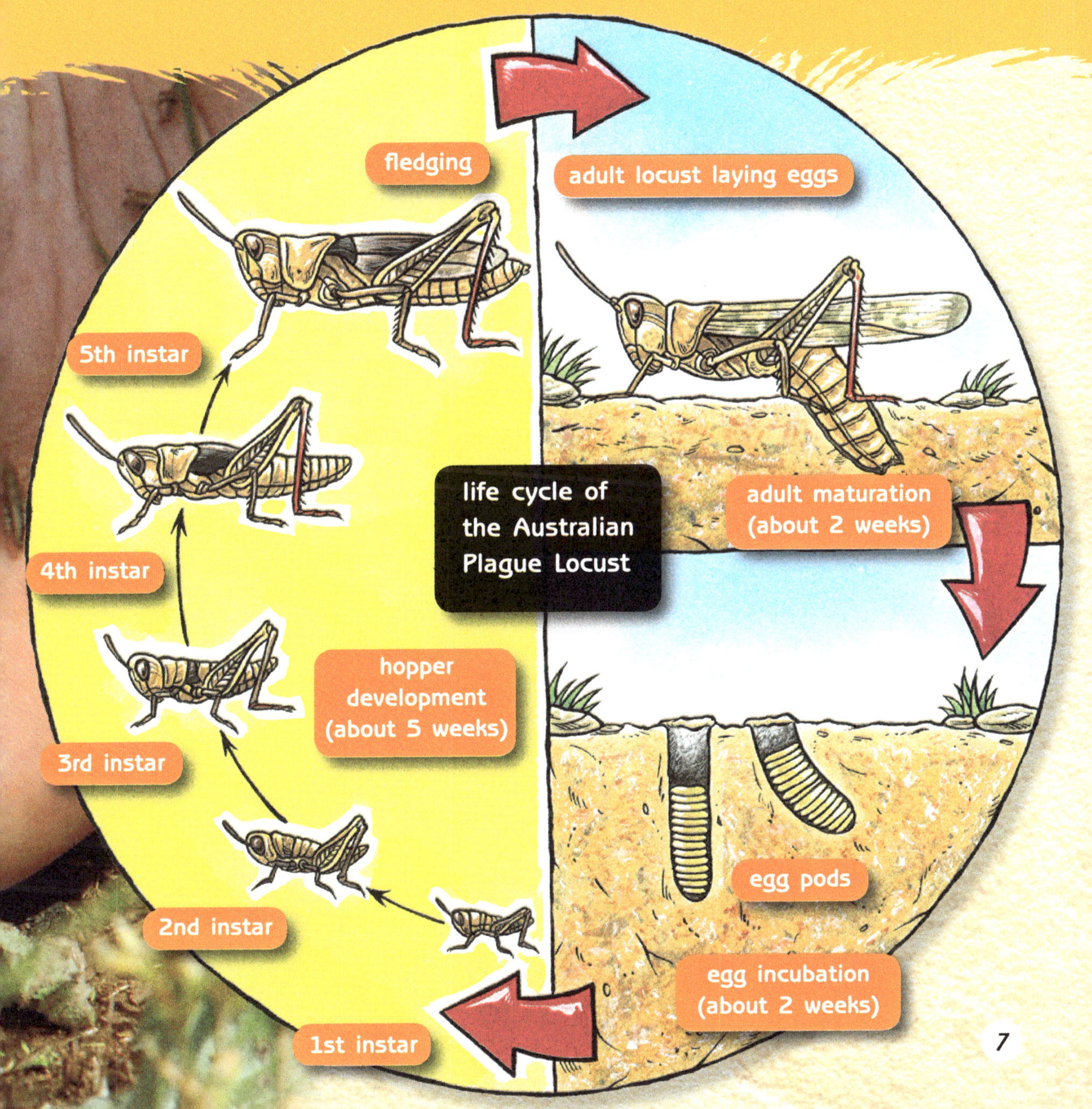

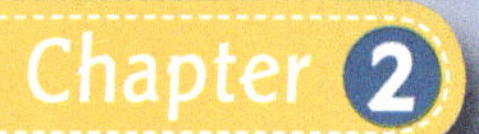

LOCUST PLAGUES

When locust numbers are low, locusts fly only short distances to feed. They do not form huge groups, or swarms, and they do not cause much damage.

When locust numbers are high, locusts group together in swarms. Swarms fly from place to place looking for food. This is called a locust plague. A locust plague can cause a lot of damage to crops, **pasture** and gardens.

Why Plagues Happen

Locust plagues can happen after a lot of rain has fallen.
After the rain, lots of green plants grow,
which locusts feed on.
Then, the female locusts lay their eggs.

female locust laying eggs in the ground

Running Words 224

If the weather stays just right
and there are plenty of green plants to eat:

- the eggs hatch quickly
- more nymphs live to become adults
- female locusts lay more eggs
- nymphs grow into adults and form swarms.

Soon, there are millions of locusts looking for food.
This is a locust plague.

Spraying Locusts

It is the job of some government workers to travel around the country looking for locusts. Farmers are also asked to report any locusts they see.

If large numbers of locusts are found, they may be sprayed with **insecticides** from aeroplanes or helicopters.

government worker collecting locusts

government worker examining locusts

Spraying from the air is not allowed in areas where lots of people live, so some spraying is done from trucks or by hand.

Locusts, like all insects, are an important part of nature. Spraying is meant to reduce the size of a plague, not to kill all locusts.

Chapter 3

OUR FARM

Dear Anne,

Thanks for your email.
It's great to have a penpal from another country.
My name is Jeff, and my family has a farm in Australia.
We grow **wheat** and other crops on our farm.
Let me tell you what happened here last week.

Until last week, our plants had been growing well because we've had a lot of rain.

Our wheat fields looked like this:

Then the locusts came.
They flew towards our farm in a swarm,
which contained millions of locusts
and covered an area of several square kilometres.
The locusts came from an area far away.
They had flown through the night.

the locust swarm arriving at night

Early the next morning, I went outside with Dad.
We looked at the swarm in the sky.
I had never seen so many animals
together at the one time.
Dad said there was nothing
we could do for the crops.
I wasn't afraid, because locusts don't hurt people.

Chapter 4

OUR FIELDS

The swarm landed in our fields,
and the locusts ate most of our wheat.
We lost a lot of our **harvest**.
Then the locusts flew to other farms in our area
and ate some of those crops, too.

This is what our damaged fields looked like
when the locusts had gone.

I didn't go to school that day,
because the swarm of locusts made it hard for drivers to see on the roads and the school bus didn't run.
Instead, I helped Mum and Dad on the farm.

Chapter 5

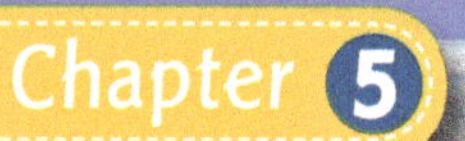

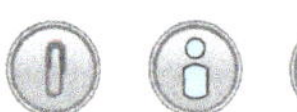

THE PLAGUE IS OVER

The locust plague is over now,
and the locusts have all gone.

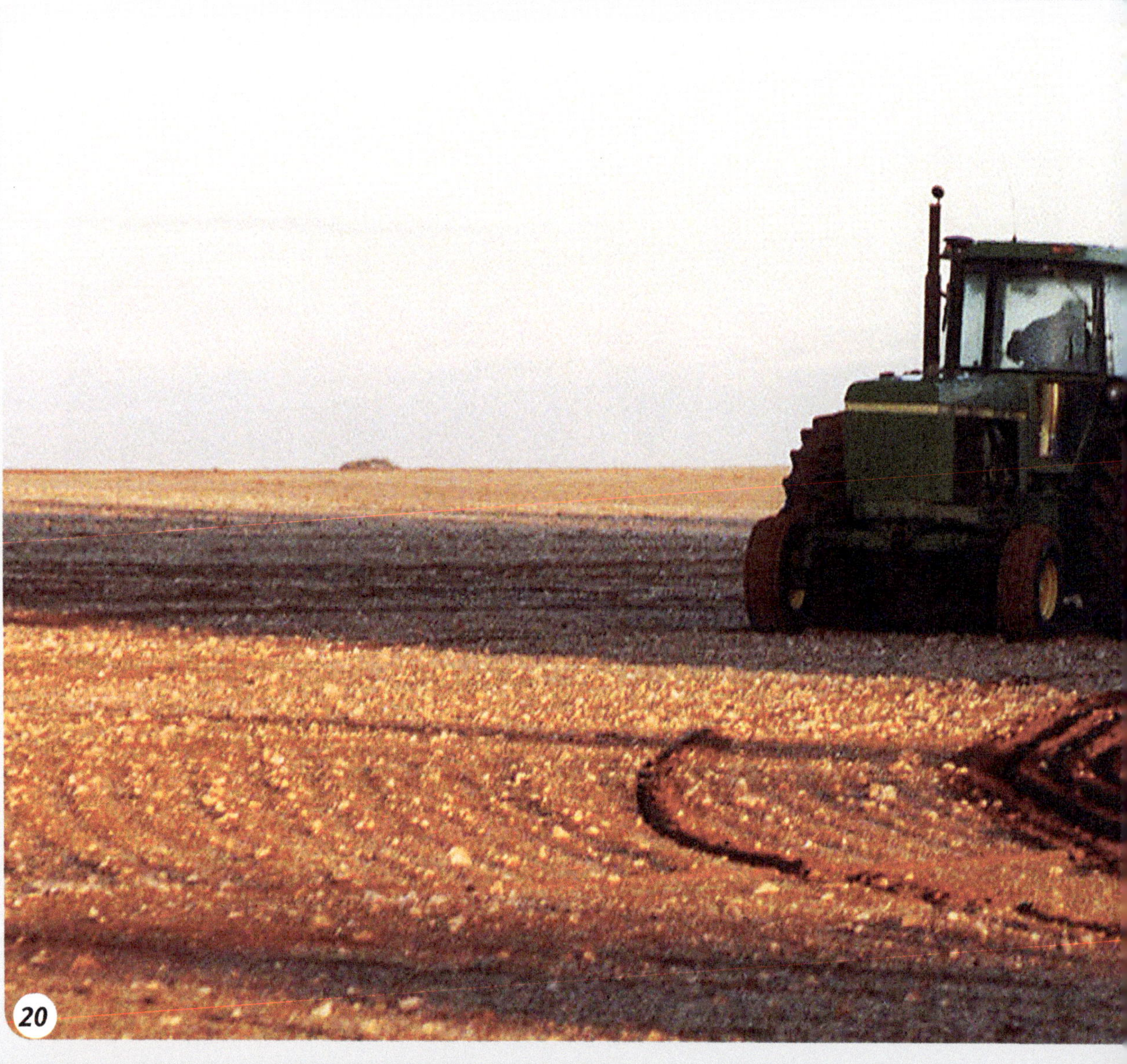

Mum and Dad said we must get
the damaged fields ready for the new plants.
We are going to be very busy on the farm.

Email me again soon.

Your new friend,
Jeff

Chapter 6

FACTS ABOUT LOCUSTS

P.S. Here are some interesting facts about locusts:

1. The most famous species is the desert locust.
   It is found in parts of Africa and Asia.

a desert locust

2. In some countries,
   people catch locusts in huge nets,
   then cook and eat them.

3. Many larger animals, like lizards, feed on locusts during a locust plague.
However, they cannot eat enough
to make much difference to locust numbers.

Glossary

harvest a crop

insecticides special chemicals that are used to kill insects

nymph a baby locust

pasture land covered with plants that farm animals feed on

species a group of plants or animals that are the same

wheat a plant used to make flour

wing pads the area on a locust where the wings grow

Index